SPELLRAISER

Tim Hawken

with illustrations by Sofia Behnke

Seahawk
Press

For those who still believe in magic...

Foreword

Spellraiser is made up of 100 chapters of exactly 100 words.

While a 100-word micro story is called a drabble, I'm not sure what a novelette like this is called. A rabble, maybe?

Despite the lack of a formal name, here it is.

For those sticklers out there who feel like they want to count the words in each chapter to make sure I'm not cheating, have at it. Just note that I've gone with software's convention of counting hyphenated words as being singular, e.g. first-class is one word, rather than two.

This intro, weirdly, is also 100 words. Fun.

1

Saint Lucius' Secondary College. Or as I called it, Lucifer's. Hell on earth.

Society's rich roses enjoyed a first-class education here. Facilities second to none. Teachers trained to bring forth the best.

Then, there were the thorns - me and Meg. The poor on scholarships. Teased mercilessly as second-class citizens.

Mostly, we kept our heads down, letting the elite enjoy their 80s Eden of perms and perfume.

If we stuck to the library and didn't try to move up the vine, all was tolerable. Just.

Until the roses started turning up dead, and everyone at school thought that I'd done it.

2

The first funeral was held on a Tuesday. Canon Cox gave the service, looking more movie star than school chaplain.

I watched him closely while I held Meg's hand. She'd dressed typical goth - enough eyeshadow to blind a panda.

Cox described Sophie as a model student.

"She bloomed not long ago on her sixteen birthday."

Now she was fertiliser.

No one watched Cox. They had eyes on me. Whispers on their lips.

Sophie and I had fought last week. I'd looked at her boyfriend sideways.

"What are we doing for your sixteenth?" Meg murmured, helping distract me from the gossip.

3

Sophie's body looked ugly in its coffin. I shouldn't say that about the dead, but it was true.

In the last few months she'd gone from plain to impossibly divine. Her eyes sparkled. Her nails glittered... even when they scratched me.

Now, she'd gone dull again, like the departing of her spirit took her newfound spark with it.

I cried looking at her. She was so young. Even if she was mean, Sophie didn't deserve this.

Canon Cox met my eyes.

"It's okay to cry, Lily" he said. "If you ever need to talk with more than tears, I'm here."

4

A week of classes turned sadness into routine. The school moved on it seemed.

Meg and I went to Camden Market on the weekend. We tried on tartan and chains. I pined over an antique box that the stall holder said belonged to a witch.

On Monday, the world felt right again, gossip forgotten.

Meg ran her fingers through my hair in the library, teasing I should dye its beautiful red to black. An ongoing joke.

Then, from nowhere, a girl, Tracey, cracked the back of my head with a book. My nose slammed on the table.

"Murderer," she said.

5

Blood oozed onto my lips, down my chin.

I sat, shocked.

"I know it was you," Tracey said. "I've got proof."

Meg leapt to my defense. She grabbed Tracey's pristine shirt. Was about to slap the bully's pimply face when the librarian stepped in.

"Girls, this isn't ladylike!" he said, all horn-rimmed glasses and tweed.

"Lucky we're not ladies then," Meg said, swinging.

Crack!

Tracey went sprawling. Her philosophy book/weapon tumbled to the floor.

The librarian bundled Meg up before she could hit again.

I still sat, dumb.

All I could think was: *why is Thick Tracey reading Nietzsche?*

6

Meg was hauled to the principal. Tracey, pampered by staff.

I was left alone to contemplate if I wanted to stay at the school or 'find somewhere more suited to my station in life.'

I dabbed my bloody nose with a tissue. No silk hankies for me.

Maybe leaving would be better, but there was no way I'd give these snobs the satisfaction.

Meg didn't come back that day - suspended for a week.

Tracey didn't come back either. Or the next day. Or next.

She was found hanging from a tree in a private garden between school and home. Dead.

7

Police didn't know if it was suicide or murder. Either way, the circumstances were suspicious.

Meg and I were hauled in for questioning. The cops didn't have a clue - literally. No marks left at the scene. There'd been none at Sophie's death either.

We were cut loose from their interview rooms back to the prison of Lucifer's.

Where the police presumed innocence, students knew who was guilty.

Tracey and Sophie's friends spat on us, exiled us, more than we'd been already.

The worst were Dhalia the Rich and Eric the Filthy Rich.

They said they'd have us killed in revenge.

8

A week of torment. Two.

At least there were no more dead bodies.

The cops had come up with doughnuts. Zero.

Meg and I huddled in our library fortress. She was sure it would all blow over. Was planning a birthday party for me.

"Fancy black cake or 'noir'?" she asked.

Then, a shadow fell on us.

It was Marcus Halifax. Sophie's boyfriend. Tall. Sad blue eyes. Brown hair. Painfully handsome in his melancholy.

Until now, he'd left us alone.

I braced for an assault.

"I know you didn't do it," he said instead. "And, I'd like to prove it."

9

Marcus sat down between Meg and I. He smelled of fresh sweat and cinnamon.

Suddenly I was hungry. I looked away, anywhere but him.

Marcus cleared his throat. Meg glared at the both of us.

"Sophie said she was being followed," Marcus murmured.

That got my attention.

"Why haven't you told the police?" Meg snapped.

"I've told anyone who might listen. No one will."

"Why?" I asked.

"Because Soph said it was a 'shadowman' and it wanted to steal her beauty."

Silence. No one listened to crazy talk.

"The strange thing is," Marcus whispered. "Now her makeup box is gone."

10

Marcus drew a picture of Sophie's makeup box. It had an eye on the lid.

"Sophie's parents deny it exists," Marcus said. "But it was her birthday present from them. It's like I'm going mad. Then, there's Tracey."

"Thick Tracey?" Meg asked.

I shot her a dark glance. We shouldn't call her that anymore.

"Everyone knew she wasn't the smartest," Marcus said slowly, "but she just passed her A-Levels. Was aiming for early university."

"What?!" I asked. "How?"

"That's all I know," Marcus shrugged. "Two mysteries. Two deaths. Could you help me dig deeper?"

"Yes," I whispered.

"No," Meg said.

11

Meg wouldn't help get to the bottom of things, but I needed to.

I knocked on Canon Cox's door. His office was cluttered with books and cheesy aphorisms like 'God's Power Is In You!'.

"How are you holding up?" he asked as I entered.

"I came to ask about Tracey."

"Tracey?" Cox frowned.

"Did she really pass A-Levels?"

Cox folded his arms.

"I can't talk about other students."

Then, I saw it. One of his books' spines had the same eye design as Sophie's makeup box.

Had *he* done it?

I left without another word.

"Lily!" Cox called after me.

12

I didn't feel safe at school. I didn't feel safe at home. The Canon knew where I lived after all.

Instead, I called a meeting at Camden Market. The stalls and oddities somehow calmed me. The public space meant nobody would hurt me there.

"Don't jump to conclusions," Meg said after I'd told her and Marcus about the book. "The Canon is the kindest man I know."

This didn't sound like Meg. My raised eyebrow told her so.

"He's been helping me," Meg said looking down.

"There's definitely something fishy there though," Marcus pressed. "I think we need that book."

13

Night. Black except for the yellow of our torches.

Marcus crept through Saint Lucifer's with me. Meg had refused to come. She'd been suspended once already. Expulsion was out of the question.

I tried the door of the Canon's office. Unlocked. Thieves' luck was with us.

Quickly, we searched the bookshelves. The eye book and its answers had to be somewhere.

A minute felt like an age. My heart slammed in my chest. Thud, thud, thud.

Marcus seemed calmer. Still, he couldn't find it.

Thud.

Not my heart this time. The door.

"Odd hour for a visit," the Canon said.

14

Cox smiled a killer smile, raising a dark object in his hand.

He flicked on the light.

We shrank back like vampires from sunshine.

"Coffee?" he asked, giving the Thermos he held a shake. "I'd offer whiskey but I might get in trouble."

Casually, Cox moved around us, sat down and poured himself a cup.

"Now. Why would two of Saint Lucius' finest be here so late?"

"For answers," Marcus said.

Cox nodded, selecting a book from his shelf. He handed it to me.

"Every question you have is answered here."

I looked down. No eye. It was the bible.

15

The bible proved useless. Like Canon Cox, it waved away serious enquiry with vague advice and outdated world views.

Cox hadn't reported us though. He'd continued to offer counseling in our troubled time—an infuriating picture of understanding.

Meg said 'I told you so' a thousand times and told us to drop it. The police had hit dead ends. Why did we think it was up to us to solve things?

So, I dropped it. She was my friend, I should listen. Better to move on.

Unfortunately others hadn't.

On Friday outside school, Eric the Filthy Rich cornered me.

Alone.

16

Eric pushed me into the shadows between two buildings. His glib grin carried rank breath beneath, like a fetid breeze from a newly painted dumpster.

I backed down the alley. There was a rusted fence behind me. The only way out would be through him.

"Eric," I said. "I had nothing to do with Sophie or Tracey."

"Liar," he said, still smiling.

For a moment, his eyes flashed with tiny black veins.

I would have gasped but he gripped me by the throat, lifting me off the ground, impossibly strong.

He held me there as I choked, my feet dangling.

17

I kicked but couldn't scream. The pressure of Eric's hand around my windpipe was silent death. His fingernails broke my skin. Blood trickled down my neck.

Eric didn't even break a sweat. He just smiled, studying me with his hideous, veined eyes.

Stars fluttered around my vision. Black closed in. My lungs burned hellfire.

Then, a thump. Eric let me go. I dropped to the ground like a cheap handbag.

Another body dropped beside me. Eric's?

I struggled for consciousness.

A pair of arms lifted me gently. Fresh sweat and cinnamon filled my nostrils.

Then, my world collapsed to night.

18

I woke in a soft bed, head aching, throat stinging.

Marcus was there, waiting. He looked up as I groaned.

"Don't get up," he said.

I glanced around. The room dripped wealth. A gold clock on the wall was worth more than my mum's car.

"How?" I began.

"Eric attacked you," Marcus said. "Lucky I was on my way to cricket," he added, twisting his bat in his hands.

Marcus was dressed in all white. What a ridiculous sport.

"I was too scared to tell anyone," Marcus said. "Did you see Eric's eyes?"

The black image came back. A monster.

19

Once I felt okay, Marcus took me home. He gave me one of his mother's scarves to wear around my neck, hiding the bruising.

My own mum gave me a sideways glance as we walked in. Marcus introduced himself. I said we were doing homework together.

She didn't buy it, but she didn't say anything either. Best mum ever.

"I think you should be 'sick' for the remaining week," Marcus said once in my room, "Until I can make sure it's safe."

"No chance," I said, resolutely. "We need to find out what Eric is, aside from a complete tosser."

20

Eric was a gentleman on the surface. He ignored me and opened doors for all the other girls. He called Marcus, 'old chum'. His eyes were back to their normal ice blue.

I was beginning to think I imagined the whole thing. The marks under my scarf reminded me otherwise.

Meg reminded me too. "They're all monsters beneath," she said. "Even Marcus. Stay away from him."

"But he helped me," I argued.

"That's what he wants you to think," she said.

Marcus passed me conspiratorial notes in the hall. Said he might be onto something.

He'd tell me this weekend.

21

I'd totally forgotten it was my birthday. Mum made me breakfast.

Meg surprised me with a gift—the antique 'witch's' box I'd loved at the market.

I hugged Meg with all I had. Best friends are the ones who take notice.

I couldn't open the lid, so we put it aside for the moment. We listened to music, chatted with mum.

Then, a knock. Marcus's face at the door.

"Is this a party?" Mum asked.

"A party crasher," Meg folded her arms.

I let him in. He smiled at mum, frowned at Meg.

"We need to talk," he said. "Upstairs?"

22

Marcus wanted to speak alone. Meg insisted she come. She brought my new box, holding it like a rock to cave his head in.

"Canon Cox is following Eric," Marcus said as the door closed.

"Are you sure?" Meg and I asked together.

"I first noticed at wrestling practice. Eric beat everyone, easily. Cox watched the whole time. He was there at lunch too, then science, then after school all the way home. All week."

"So you're stalking Cox, who's stalking Eric?" Meg said.

"I think Eric may be in danger."

"Good," Meg said.

I couldn't feel much sympathy either.

23

We argued all afternoon.

Should we go to the police? Confront Cox?

And say what?

"This is hopeless." I slumped onto my bed.

"Hopeless like this box lid," Meg said, trying to open it again. "It's almost as stubborn as you, Lily."

I poked my tongue at her.

"Here," Marcus said.

He strained. No use. That satisfied Meg.

"Maybe a spell opens it," she grinned. "It belonged to a witch, you know?"

Marcus rolled his eyes.

"Let's do a summoning!" she said.

"This isn't the time," I sighed.

"Come on," Meg insisted. "What's a sixteenth birthday party without a seance?"

24

Meg took an hour to prepare. Candles. Chalk. Incense.

It was actually a fun distraction seeing Marcus squirm.

As twilight fell, Meg placed the box in her 'witch's circle'.

"Oh dark lord," she said seriously. "We ask you to raise forth a spirit and open this unholy receptacle."

Nothing happened.

"Oh Senpai," Meg continued. "Hear our passionate call."

She raised her hands. Nothing.

"Here," I said, taking Meg's place. "Spirits, spirits, come out and play."

I tried the lid.

"Please," I added.

The box opened. Stunned silence.

Then, with a hissing thwack, a rush of air thundered into my chest.

25

I gasped to my feet, my hand on my heart. It felt like my ribcage would burst.

Marcus and Meg jumped up too. They rushed to my side, holding me up on unsteady feet.

"What was that?!" Marcus asked.

Meg watched me, wide eyed.

I laughed then. It bubbled up from nowhere. A full-throated expression of joy.

But it wasn't me laughing.

My friends stepped back.

Relief washed over them.

"Oh babe," Meg smiled. "You had me going for a second there!"

Marcus looked down at the box.

"It's empty," he said.

It is now, I thought. *It is now.*

26

Meg and Marcus left, thinking I'd played a great joke on them. That I'd managed to get the box open somehow and faked the sense that something happened.

I didn't try to convince them otherwise. I didn't tell them my entire body was sparking with electricity from the inside out. I didn't tell them something was wrong.

Because, somehow, everything felt right, like I was becoming something *more*.

And so, I let them leave with promises to be careful about Eric and Cox. To keep an eye out for anything strange.

They didn't know that 'strange' was just the beginning.

27

I walked into school the next day, charged and confident. Manic energy had taken ahold. I knew I'd get to the bottom of things somehow.

I breezed past the peering faces. Who cared what they thought?

Marcus spotted me from a distance.

His voice jumped into my mind. *She's so unique,* it said.

I was startled but remained calm. All normal. All cool. I waved coyly. He smiled.

Then, I saw Eric.

I was an idiot to hurt her, his voice whispered.

I narrowed my eyes. Eric looked away, red faced.

What was happening?

Whatever it was, I liked it.

28

It was the best day I'd ever had at Lucifer's.

I instinctively knew every teacher's question. Sidestepped conflict through sixth sense.

That box had given me the power to read people. If a thought was strong enough, I'd actually hear the words.

I had to find Cox. He couldn't hide behind vague deflections now.

But, he wasn't in his office or the library. Was he below, in the prohibited crypts maybe? Lucifer's used to be a gothic cathedral.

I spotted Meg.

"Have you seen Cox?" I asked.

"No," her mouth said.

What's wrong with Lily's eyes? her thoughts said instead.

29

"What about Eric then?" I asked, brushing Meg's thought away.

Meg shook her head, as much to say "no" as to clear her own mind it seemed.

She's fine. I must be seeing things, her silent voice told me.

"I think I've figured out how to get to the bottom of everything," I said.

"Oh yeah?" she asked, waiting for more.

Just then, I saw them. Eric strolled down a far corridor. Cox shadowed behind.

"I'll explain later," I said to Meg hurriedly and rushed after them.

My friend's anxiety followed after me, even though she stayed where she was.

30

As I burst from the school, Eric drove off in a town car. Was it already the end of the day? I'd been too engrossed in my own head to take notice.

Cox was getting into his little black Escort.

"Canon!" I called.

He looked back, then at the road, torn.

I ran forward. I couldn't lose this chance. I had to be direct.

Cox stood half in his car behind its door.

"Why are you following Eric?" I asked.

He had no words, but an image shot into my mind. Something so terrifying, the whole world fell into darkness.

31

Tracey hung from the tree, her eyes lifeless.

Her hands reached down like she was stretching for something.

Why wasn't she grasping up at the rope? Was there something more important?

There was nothing on the ground.

Where was it?

Then, sirens.

Back in the present, all was silent. Tracey was gone. So was Cox.

I blinked the vision away. Cox's car disappeared down the street. He'd gotten away.

I had to go to that park.

What had Tracey been reaching for as she hung there?

The police had found nothing, but maybe I would with this new sixth sense.

32

I slipped through the gates of the private park.

The tree from my vision stood in the middle, reaching with its dark branches to a grey sky.

My mind flashed to Tracey hanging. Swinging.

The vision had been from Cox's point of view. He must have done it. Must've wanted whatever Tracey had.

I searched the ground. Nothing. Surely there had to be *some* clue. I kept looking. Just footprints and despair.

The sun set. I had no choice but to leave.

Whispers followed me home. Thoughts from passersby. Personal paranoia. It was hard to separate everything.

I needed sleep.

33

I woke the next morning with clear purpose but a muddled mind.

I needed to find what was in that park. But how? Whatever had been there was long gone.

Maybe I could tell Meg. Would she think I was crazy? How could I explain the visions?

Perhaps Marcus would listen.

I got ready for school, lost in a brain fog.

Mum tried to talk to me over breakfast, but her inner thoughts drowned out her verbal words.

Other whispers followed me walking to school.

Then, those whispers started screaming.

Cox was waiting for me. And, Meg was with him.

34

I ducked behind a tree. Neither Meg nor Cox had seen me.

The same frantic thought came to me again and again, my whispers telling me what the two wanted.

We have to get her alone.

But Meg was supposed to be my friend! She'd had my back since the first day of school, holding my trembling hand at assembly to calm me.

My whispers insisted. *Meg told you Cox was nice. To stop snooping. She's part of it.*

I struggled to separate my own thoughts from what was coming to me.

Then, something bubbled up, deep and clear.

Run.

35

I ran without looking back. Did they see me?

I couldn't go home. Meg would search Camden Market.

I went to Marcus's. Rattled the gates. Shouted. No answer.

Then, my whispers made me stop. A woman watched me from across the street.

What's up with that girl? I better call the police.

I was making a scene.

I slinked away, staying in the shadows, always moving.

I eventually came to the private park.

Look under the tree, I thought.

I tried, but couldn't. My brain was a twisted jumble.

Then, a voice. Spoken, not thought.

"There you are," Cox said.

36

I turned to escape but Meg was behind me. Something square was in her hand.

My whispers hissed at it.

"Pin her down," Cox ordered.

"No!" I spun, clawing at him with sudden rage.

Cox grabbed my wrist, twisted.

I sunk to my knees.

"Get her!" he yelled.

Meg's hands were on me. So many hands.

They forced me down.

"Out, by the power of God. Get out." Cox mumbled.

No! My whispers screamed back.

"Never," a voice growled from inside me.

"Out!" Cox commanded, bringing his hand to my chest.

It felt like he was ripping out my soul.

37

My back arched. My throat constricted. My eyes bugged wide.

A torrent of sensation rushed out of me.

"Inside!" Cox said forcefully.

He pointed to a familiar box Meg now held above me. Something smacked inside. The lid snapped shut.

All went still.

I lay there, panting, heaving. I was alive. It felt like I'd just burst up from underwater.

Realising, I looked at Cox and scrambled backward, afraid.

"It's okay," Meg said soothingly behind me.

"Cox killed her," I managed. "Tracey. I saw it."

"No, child," Cox soothed. "But I hold myself responsible. It's time you learned the truth."

38

"You were possessed," Cox said from across his desk.

We sat in his office, me still shaken, Meg close at my side.

"That box you stumbled upon is called a Spellkeeper," Cox continued.

"You what?" I asked, struggling even with the word *possessed*.

"Spells are like spirits," Cox continued patiently. "Invite them inside, they give you powers."

I thought of Sophie's sudden beauty.

Tracey's newfound intelligence.

Tracey was reaching for something as she hung. Her... Spellkeeper?

"If you keep spells in too long they take control of you. Possess you." Cox said. "And, they're so rare, people kill for them."

39

Meg and I sat stunned.

"It's a lot to take in, I know" Canon Cox echoed my thoughts. He scribbled something on a notepad. "You'll find a full explanation in this book in the library."

"Library?" Meg scoffed.

It was our haven. If there were books about magic in there, we'd know.

Cox handed me the piece of paper. The title made me laugh despite myself.

Latin Translations of Ancient Greek Myths.

No wonder we'd never noticed it. No student in their right mind would check that out.

"Until you read it, I'm holding onto your Spellkeeper, Lily" Cox said.

40

No amount of arguing convinced Cox to give the box back.

I felt oddly incomplete without it, like the spirit left a hole that needed filling. The book we read in the library listed that as a common 'side effect'.

There were more horrors if you didn't take the 'spell' out regularly. Your eyes turned black. You became 'Fallen', controlled by your spell instead of you controlling it. It meant other 'Spellraisers' could control you too.

I remembered Eric's eyes, almost black. Remembered how Sophie described her stalker as a Shadowman.

Had someone become Fallen and was now hunting others?

41

The Librarian wouldn't let us check out the book for further reading. It had been a long day. I needed to go home, rest, but I wanted to keep learning.

"Sorry," he said, adjusting his horn-rimmed glasses. "It's part of our special collection. You're only allowed to read it here. Your name even goes on the register." He tapped a notebook.

"C'mon, Mr Lombardi, you know us, we'll look after it," I said.

"Rules are rules," he said, "I'm in early tomorrow if you're that enamoured with Latin translations." He laughed.

It was absurd.

But, we'd be in first thing.

42

Marcus tried to call that night. I told mum I was too tired.

She looked at me, like "have you guys had a lover's tiff?"

I didn't need a spell in me to read her mind there.

I didn't know how to approach Marcus though. Tell him his girlfriend had been gifted a magic box and been murdered for it? It sounded barmy.

Cox had warned us not to tell anyone either. There was some Order that governed the knowledge and use of spells. Reveal their secrets and true hell could break loose.

I needed to keep reading that book.

43

Meg and I sat hunched over the book.

The library was deserted, apart from Lombardi.

We sped through information. Spells could give you a whole catalogue of powers.

Spellraiser Trainers had 'compulsion spells' to help apprentices learn skills, but they could also be used to control other people.

I wondered if Cox had one.

Serious rules surrounded using spells too. Only proper initiates were gifted them. Sixteen was the perfect age, because you had more control of your body then. Spells *had* to be removed daily.

I was just getting to a new section when Eric strode in, looking furious.

44

Meg and I cringed back into the corner.

Eric walked up to the librarian, murmuring something we didn't hear.

Lombardi shook his head, indicating towards us.

Eric looked our way and narrowed his regular-blue eyes, a look of angry entitlement on his face.

We locked gazes, me a deer in the headlights.

Meg was calm beside me though.

"He just wants to read the book," she whispered, raising her middle finger at Eric, smiling like, *it's our turn, prick.*

Eric flexed his jaw. Took a step our way.

Then, the bell rang. Saved. Class time.

Eric glared again but left.

45

Meg had to go to science.

I had home economics. A time waster. Anyone who couldn't cook mashed potato by the time they were sixteen was going to fail at life. Unless they had money.

Eric would be there. Marcus too. No way I could go.

Instead, I went to see Cox.

He almost bumped into me on the way out of his office.

I noted the bag on his shoulder. "Off somewhere?

He paused.

"A shadowman is following Eric."

Cox let that sink in.

"I need to speak with The Order. Ask them for help. Ask to train you."

46

I stood in the hallway, watching Cox go.

He'd left me. Left Eric. Told me to watch the wanker. To look after him.

Me!

"Everything I can teach you without permission is in that book," Cox had said. "I have to go. Two students are dead already. Eric is at risk. The Order doesn't just have a phone number or postal address. I have to go in person. I still have your Spellkeeper, so you should be safe."

Great sense of security that was.

If we were lucky, Cox would be back before the 'shadowman' struck again.

We weren't lucky.

Marcus stalked the halls at lunch, searching for me.

I hid. There was too much happening to explain the impossible right now.

I had to find Meg. I had to find Eric.

I found them together.

Eric was wrestling in the gym, while Meg watched in the shadows.

I sidled up next to her. "What you up to?"

Meg jumped, hissing. "You scared me. I wanted to see if Eric's up to something dodgy."

"Is he?"

"Fighting for pleasure is always dodgy," she said.

I told her about Cox leaving.

"Shite!" Meg said.

Yup, that just about summed it up.

48

We trailed Eric the rest of the day. I got close enough at one point to check his eyes.

They definitely weren't black. He must've left his spell in too long that first time he attacked me, but had somehow been able to take it out again before becoming Fallen. That must be part of the extra training Cox alluded to.

School finished.

I slunk at a distance behind Eric, checking he was safe.

He turned down a lesser-used corridor.

Then, a shadow flickered in front of him and he was gone.

No!

I started running. This couldn't be happening.

49

I sprinted down the corridor, looking left and right for Eric. Nothing.

My breath was ragged. I should have waited for Meg to help. I could feel myself panicking.

Then, a hand shot out from behind some lockers, pulling me roughly into the shadows.

I tried to scream, but strong fingers cupped over my lips.

Squirming, I tried to get a look at my attacker. No use. The Shadowman had me.

Then a face emerged, lips sneering.

"What you following me for, slag?" Eric snarled.

His eyes were still blue. I realised then, he wasn't really angry.

Eric was terrified.

50

"Cox." I panted, when Eric took his hand from my mouth. "He asked me to make sure you were safe."

"I can look after myself!" Eric snapped. But, his fear told another story. "People like you shouldn't be involved in this."

People like me?

I wanted to punch him, but forced myself to stay civil.

"How'd you disappear like that?" I asked.

Silence.

"I thought your spell made you stronger?" I pressed.

"I've got two boxes," he said proudly.

Of course he did. Eric the Filthy Rich.

"Leave me alone," he said, stomping away.

But my conscience wouldn't let me.

51

"Let the dickhead hang," Meg said as we sat in my room talking about it.

The image of Tracey in the tree leapt into my mind.

"He's an idiot, but he doesn't deserve that," I said. I couldn't believe I was defending Eric. "We need to keep him safe."

"Oh and how we gunna do that?" Meg asked, picking her black-lacquered nails. "We've got no powers of our own and he's avoiding us worse than this 'shadow'."

I sat and stared. She was right.

"Shall we ask Marcus to help?"

Meg snorted. Yeah right.

We really were on our own.

52

I took the morning shift. Eric dodged me most of the time, but at least I could see he was alive.

Meg watched during lunch, while I studied the book some more. Apparently you could hold up to three spells in you at a time. Any more than that and you could burn up, like, literally.

I was late for the after school watch. Eric was marching down the road just as I made it outside.

I tried to follow, but another person stepped in front of me. One I'd been avoiding.

"Why won't you answer my calls?" Marcus asked.

53

Marcus looked at me with hurt eyes. I wanted to hug him, but this wasn't the time to melt under a puppy-dog gaze.

Eric was already halfway to the corner.

"I can't…" I said, walking away, down Lucifer's front steps.

"Can't what?" Marcus followed.

"Just…" I didn't know what.

Marcus blocked my path.

"What's up?" he pleaded. "What's going on with you? With everything?"

"You wouldn't understand," I started.

"Try me," Marcus said.

I didn't get a chance to reply.

Down the street, there was a screech of tyres and a deafening bang.

A car had plowed right into Eric.

54

Screams. Marcus was already running toward the accident.

People pointed, gasping. Others rushed from their cars to help.

None of them made any difference. Eric was dead, his brain leaking onto the road.

Marcus was doing CPR when I got there. No one tried to stop him, even though everyone could see it was hopeless.

People whispered that the car that hit Eric was empty. It was abandoned on the curb, door open, no driver.

There was something else only I seemed to notice too.

Eric's school bag lay turned inside-out on the road. Someone had taken his spell boxes.

55

"The Order aren't sending any help."

I thought Cox was joking. Surely three murders was an emergency.

"There's a more pressing matter in Ireland," he explained. "Terrorists have gotten their hands on some Spellkeepers."

"And what about training me?"

"They don't want uninitiated families using magic. This Ireland thing has them even more on edge."

"Wait. So poor people can't be trusted?!" I stood, my voice rising too. "I'm more determined and work harder than any silver-spoon prat."

Cox looked deflated. "There's more. A cloaking spell I didn't know about went missing here last year. Our suspect could be anyone."

56

By the time I made it home, my anger had been replaced with despair.

Cox was still holding my Spellkeeper so I wouldn't be a target.

I was literally powerless. Just another useless teenager unable to change an unjust world.

"What's up, sweetheart?" Mum asked as I slumped at the table. "That boy's accident still on your mind?"

"Something like that," I mumbled.

She gave me a hug. "Well, this'll cheer you up. Marcus called. He said to tell you his parents gave him a makeup box for his birthday. Isn't that funny? A boy like him being given makeup?"

57

Meg and I rattled Marcus's gate.

"Thought that'd get your attention," he said through the intercom.

We went to his room without speaking more. I wanted to say I was sorry. That I hadn't wanted to confuse him.

He spoke first instead.

"So this is why the others were killed. For magic." he said, indicating an oak-colored Spellkeeper on his bed. "But, you'd figured that out already, hadn't you?"

I nodded.

"I was worried you'd think I'd gone nuts," I said.

He held up his hand for me to stop.

"I need to know. Are you guys doing the killings?"

58

"What?" I blurted. "Are you kidding?"

Meg simply glared.

Marcus unbuttoned his shirt, fury smoldering in his eyes.

"If you are, then stab me now." He bared his chest. "Use the scissors on the dresser. I don't want to live in a world where I can't trust my friends."

His words cut worse than any scissors could. I'd let him down. Betrayed him with my silence.

Behind me, Meg went to the dresser. The scissors scraped as she picked them up.

She went to the window, throwing them out.

"Button up, Romeo," she said. "We've got some thinking to do."

59

We sat, debating for hours. In the end, there was one conclusion.

"It *has* to be Cox," I said. "No one else knows who all the students with boxes are."

Meg shook her head for the fiftieth time.

"It can't be him. Cox helped you get that spell out before it claimed you as Fallen."

"Exactly," I said. "And now he's taken it for himself without suspicion. I bet he pretended he was away while killing Eric too. An alibi he knows full well we can't check."

"There's only one way to know for sure," Marcus said. "We confront him."

60

"This is crazy," I said, marching through school with Marcus and Meg.

"No more sneaking around," Marcus said. "Keeping secrets has done nothing but let people die."

"But uncovering this secret might get *us* killed," Meg said.

"I'll protect you," Marcus said.

Meg's eyebrows raised so quickly they almost flew off her forehead. "Don't be a git."

"You don't understand," he said. "My spell makes me impervious to weapons. I already have it in."

I remembered his chest. The scissors.

"So much for trusting friends," I said.

Still, I didn't blame him.

We neared Cox's office. The moment of truth.

61

Cox raised a gun at us from behind his desk when we opened the door.

Marcus stepped forward as a shield.

Cox smiled, clicking the gun's safety back on.

"You startled me," he said. "I thought you were the killer coming for my Spellkeeper."

"You mean *my* Spellkeeper?" I snapped.

"Yours too," he said. "I hoped both would be enough of a lure. But, whoever it is either doesn't know I have them, or is too scared to face me."

"Prove you're not the killer," Meg demanded.

"How can I if you don't trust me?"

"I know how," I said.

62

I pointed to my Spellkeeper, which sat on Cox's bookshelf behind him.

"Let me use that to read your thoughts," I said.

"You know I can't do that," Cox frowned, "The Order -"

"Stuff The Order," Meg cut in.

Cox looked genuinely shocked.

"You said they've just left us to deal with it, *if* you're telling the truth," I continued. "Well, this is us dealing with it."

Cox stared at us for a long time. Resigned, he finally nodded.

I grabbed my box hungrily and opened it. Waited.

Nothing happened.

"You have to invite it in," Cox sighed. "Just be careful."

63

The spell shivered into me.

It felt like what I imagined sleeping with Marcus might be like. Intimate. Exquisite.

But I had to concentrate.

Whispers ambushed my mind. Meg's thoughts. Marcus's emotions. Cox's fears. All swirling as one.

"Look at whoever you need to concentrate on," a clear voice said above everything. Cox.

Opening my eyes, I looked at him.

Visions strobed through me. Cox in front of two old men. Them shaking their heads. Him looking at Tracey's body. The vision went blurry and sadness gripped me. I was looking through Cox's tears.

"Stop," I sobbed. "Make it stop."

65

"Discedo!" Cox said forcefully.

With a whoosh, the spirit left me, clattering into the Spellkeeper on the desk.

I stumbled backward. Meg and Marcus steadied me.

"What was that?" I gasped.

Cox gave a tight smile. "That was me exorcising your spell. It's easier when it hasn't gotten its hooks into you."

The emptiness inside me ached.

"So, he didn't do it?" Meg asked.

I shook my head.

"Then who did?" Marcus echoed my thoughts.

We all stood, silent.

Then, Cox's face hardened.

"We're going to find out," he said. "You're right. Stuff the Order. I'm going to train you."

65

Despite his commitment to train us, Cox's rules were stifling.

No practicing without him. *Never* using a spell in public, in case the killer noticed and made us their next victim.

Meg didn't help. She was moody every time I saw her, eying my Spellkeeper like it was evil.

"Wish I'd never bought you that stupid thing," she snapped one night, when I'd been talking about how powerful I felt bonded with the spirit.

I didn't know what to say.

She got up and left.

I felt exactly like it did when I had to take out my spell. Empty.

66

As Meg and I cracked apart, Marcus and I melded together.

We had a shared secret. A shared fear.

Every day we looked over our shoulders for the killer, just as we watched each other's backs.

Mercifully, no one was following either of us. Yet.

We met one morning with Cox for our latest lesson.

"This is possibly the most important thing you could learn," he said, looking Marcus and I each in the eye.

"I'm going to teach you how to expel the spirits from each other."

"Why?" I asked.

"In case one of you turns dark," he replied.

67

Marcus and I stood across from each other, ready. It was my turn to fail.

I stepped forward, shouting "discedo!" with a force I didn't feel. It meant *leave* in Latin.

Marcus's spell didn't leave though.

"Again!" Cox said, frustrated. He'd even used his compulsion spell to assist and I'd still fizzled.

"I can't," I moaned.

"Can't or won't?" Cox asked.

I didn't answer.

"Tomorrow again, then," he said. "I want to flush out this killer soon."

"How?!" Marcus asked, alert.

"With a display of your power," Cox said. "Once they know you have a spell, they'll come after you."

68

"Why do you think we can't exorcise each other's spells?" Marcus asked as we walked through empty school halls.

We both knew why, he just wanted me to say it.

"Because we don't want to hurt each other," I said. "It feels like shite to have a spell pulled out of you."

His hand went to mine in answer. I clung onto his fingers.

"We need to practice," he sighed. "Properly."

"Your house?" I asked.

My place was impossible. Mum was always there.

"Sure," he nodded. "You want to invite Meg? We should let her know what Cox is planning."

69

Meg wasn't around. Her dad said she was studying.

Always studying. Always in the school library.

Marcus shuffled uneasily on his bed. "Again?"

I cradled my head in my hands. "Surely there have to be better skills to learn than this."

Marcus's smirk said he could make a few suggestions. Instead, he shrugged. "The ability to rob the power from an attacking Fallen would certainly come in handy."

I couldn't argue with that.

"If only we knew who it was," I sighed.

Then, it struck me. We *did* know who it was.

We just hadn't looked in the right spot.

70

Marcus and I stalked toward the school library. It was 7.30am on Monday but Mr Lombardi should be there - an early bird who got the bookworm.

"So, what's the plan?" Marcus asked.

"You distract Lombardi while I find the catalogue of who's applied to read the Spellraiser book. It should be under the counter."

"Perfect."

We entered, quiet as thieves. Lombardi was already busy in the stacks, so Marcus went to draw him deeper. I snuck behind the front desk and looked for the list, heart pounding.

But then, a creak.

"What are you doing?!" someone hissed, making me jump.

71

Meg watched me from a seat near the desk.

"Jesus! You almost gave me a heart attack," I whispered. "I need the list of who's been reading the Spellraiser book. It should be a list of suspects."

Meg narrowed her eyes, saying nothing else.

I riffled around the counter. A minute. Two. It felt like an age.

Finally, I found it. A ledger.

I'd expected a long list, but only Cox, Tracey, Sophie, Eric, Marcus and I were in there. No other options that could be the killer. Except one.

Someone who had checked the book out dozens of times…

Meg.

72

Meg approached me - all black nails, hair and eyeshadow.

I flinched back.

She stepped forward and lamp light hit her hazel eyes. Thank god. *They* weren't black.

"What's it say?" she asked.

"Nothing," I said. "But -"

"But what?" Meg whispered, looking around to make sure Lombardi wasn't coming back.

"But, your name's written in there," I said.

"'Course it is," she said. "I've been studying the book."

"Why?" was all I could think to say.

"To help," she said softly, looking at her feet.

I checked again. All the dates beside her name were recent ones. Not the killer then.

"You want to be the bait for a magical killer?" Meg snapped, now back at Marcus's place.

I shuffled unconformably at her direct response to Cox's plan.

"When you put it like that it does sound pretty reckless," I said.

Marcus crossed his arms, full of false bravado, leaning against his bookcase. "It's the only way. We'll be careful."

"You'll be carefully dead," Meg said, before turning to me. "Lily, promise you won't."

"I-"

"She doesn't have to do it," Marcus said. "I will. I've had things handed to me my whole life. It's about time I paid my dues."

74

We stood in the middle of the main hallway at school. It was empty, for now. Class was on.

"I'm not sure this is a good idea," Cox said, his regular smile a pinched frown. "I may have been too hasty."

"Relax," Meg soothed. "I actually think it's going to be kind of fun."

She'd become more excited about the plan when Marcus explained what he wanted to happen.

Marcus checked his watch. "One minute. Action stations."

We all took our positions, me holding Marcus's hand.

The bell rang.

Meg pulled a wicked-looking kitchen knife from her bag, grinning widely.

75

"I'm gunna kill you!" Meg screamed.

Students stared goggle-eyed from the doors of their classrooms.

Meg swung wildly at Marcus with the knife. He dodged, pushing me behind him.

She stabbed again. "Stay away from my friend, you cheater! Liar!"

The blade caught Marcus's arm, tearing through his blazer. Another stab. A chest blow.

People screamed. Others were frozen in horror. I saw a teacher running toward us.

As planned, Cox swept in.

"Bravo!" he clapped. "Relax everyone. They were just practicing drama. A show."

Marcus smiled and bowed. Meg laughed maniacally. Cox gave his plastic grin.

No one clapped.

76

Opinion around school was that Meg must either be the best actor ever or a proper psycho.

Cox was chastised by the principal. How could he stage something like that after everything that had happened? A Canon should be more sensitive!

Cox apologised and kept his job. It helped to have a perfect record.

Meanwhile, rumours went wild. Why was Marcus slumming it with us? Was I slut? Was Meg a closet lesbian? Like any of that should matter.

Yet, one thing genuinely troubled everyone. How had that knife shredded Marcus's blazer, yet not left a scratch on his skin?

77

It became clear someone was following Marcus a few days later.

Shadows moved when they shouldn't. The wind whispered unusual things.

I stuck by Marcus's side, trying to listen with my power in case anything happened. All I could detect, though, was a general sense of wrongness.

Meg was on edge too. As absent as she had been in the last weeks, now the three of us were inseparable. Marcus was glad for the extra company. An extra set of eyes to watch his back.

We thought we had it covered, until one night the shadows got into Marcus's home.

78

Marcus was in bed when it happened. A scuttling outside woke him. A creak in the hall made his blood run cold.

As the door of his room opened, midnight flooded inside, the darkness growing blacker.

Then something was on him, grabbing, stabbing, growling.

Marcus kicked and screamed.

His father burst in with a gun and blasted a warning shot into the roof.

All clicked instantly back to normal, like Marcus had simply awoken from a nightmare. It was no dream though.

The only thing that had saved Marcus was that he hadn't taken his invincibility spell out before sleep.

79

There's something extra horrifying about being attacked where you should normally feel safest.

Security around the Halifax mansion was fortified further. Marcus's dad went ballistic at Cox, demanding the Order do something more to protect his son.

When Cox explained he'd failed to convince the Order to help, Mr Halifax decided to make the journey himself.

Marcus retreated into paranoia. No classes. No contact with the outside world.

I had to force him to take his spell out each morning for a few brief hours while I stood guard.

Even doing that, his eyes got darker and darker each day.

80

The black cloud of psychic poison grew slowly toward Marcus's pupils. His veins pulsed with it.

Soon, he'd be Fallen.

"You have to rest more!" I pleaded. "Please, I can't watch you 24-7. I promise, you're safe at home."

"I'm not, unless my spell protects me." It sounded like the spirit was getting into his head, even as we spoke.

"Come on," I said. "What if Cox watches you at night?"

"He's in on this somehow," Marcus said.

Not this again.

I wanted to expel Marcus's spirit right then, but knew I couldn't do it.

I ran for Cox instead.

81

Cox wasn't in his office or the staffroom. He wasn't anywhere.

Desperate, I went to find Meg. She'd been reading more than anyone. She'd know what to do.

Yet, Meg wasn't anywhere either, not even the library. I scanned the halls with my power, listening for any whispers that might sound like her. Nothing.

My panic rose inside me like a creeping spell. I went to my locker to take mine out. To rest.

That's where I found the note.

I have your friend. Come to the school crypts with your spells tonight, or she'll be the next one dead.

82

Marcus still refused to take out his spell, no matter how much I begged.

"It could be a trick to get us to drop our guard," he argued back. "Don't worry, I'll be fine, we'll save her."

Would *he* be fine though? Could we save her?

There was no one else we could go to. Cox was still missing. Marcus's dad was uncontactable.

We had to go tonight.

Maybe this was the Shadowman's plan all along. Divide. Conquer.

Well, if he thought two kids would be easy targets, he was wrong.

Marcus and I were going to give him hell.

83

We broke into Lucifer's just before midnight.

No one thought to lock any of the doors inside, so it was free reign after the first lock.

The one door that was normally barred—the one to the crypts—was wide open too. Our Shadowman was expecting us.

We knew it was a trap, but how do you *not* try to help your friend?

Marcus had his dad's gun. I listened for any whispers of danger. It was as cautious as we could be.

We came to a bend in the passage. Something was blocking the way.

No, not something.

Someone.

84

I bit back a scream when I saw Cox's prone body. Marcus shone his torch revealing a pool of blood. A head wound.

We rushed to Cox's side. I checked for a pulse, expecting the worst. He was alive though, just. His breath was shallow, coming fast. His skin was clammy.

If we didn't get Cox help, he'd die.

"He's all yours, Marcus," I said softly and urgently. "I can't carry him."

I expected an argument. All I got back was silence.

As soon as I looked up, I knew something was seriously wrong.

Marcus's eyes had gone pitch black.

85

With a snarl, Marcus lunged for me. I slipped on Cox's blood. Marcus reeled to the side, blocking the tunnel behind.

Scrambling up, I looked desperately for an escape. I could go over Cox and into the Shadowman's trap, or fight my friend.

In Marcus's possessed state, he had initially forgotten the gun in his hand. Now, he looked at it vacantly, before raising it, his dark eyes trained on me.

"Give me your spell," he hissed.

I had nowhere to go. There was only one thing I could do.

"Discedo!" I commanded with all my strength.

Marcus simply laughed.

86

I watched in slow motion as Marcus started to pull the trigger.

I flinched back, expecting a shot.

Instead, there was another roar.

"Discedo!"

It wasn't me. It was Cox. He'd climbed to his knees and was leaning against the wall.

Marcus stumbled back as if struck.

"Out, demon!" Cox shouted again, the words coming from a primal place.

This time, the spell guttered from Marcus.

There was a chill in the air. The spirit had no box to return to.

It would go back into Marcus, unless…

"Come to me!" I commanded.

The impact hurled me to the floor.

87

The power inside felt like it would burst from my skin. My pores sung with the energy.

I sprung from the floor, ready for another attack. There wasn't one.

Marcus was on his knees against one wall, Cox slumped against the other.

I paused for the barest of moments, listening. There was a calling from deep blow.

Meg.

She was thinking one word on loop. *Help.*

Marcus's groan brought me back to the present.

He steadied on his feet, looking ashamed.

"Oh, god, Lily, I'm so-"

"Save it for later!" I snapped. "You get Cox help. I'm going after Meg."

88

For once in his life, Marcus actually did what he was told.

He helped Cox up, trying to rouse him again. Cox was barely holding onto consciousness though.

"Get to a phone," I said. "Call an ambulance. The police."

"I'll be right behind you," Marcus promised, his clear eyes tired but determined. "And Lily, take the gun. Be careful."

I wanted to tell him I was invincible now. That I didn't need his help anymore.

But that was wrong.

As we parted ways, fear gripped my body.

There was a good chance I would die in the next few minutes.

Meg's whispers for help grew louder in my mind as I neared the crypt. There was something underneath too. Something evil. Something subhuman.

I clutched the gun in my hand for comfort. Point and shoot, right? How hard could it be?

Sweat ran down the hollow of my spine. I was cold all over.

Candlelight shone from inside the crypt. I approached with dread. The door was propped wide open.

Inside, Meg sat in a circle of candles. She wasn't tied up. *She was smiling.*

"Hello, dear friend," she said upon seeing me. "I'm so glad you came to help."

92

I wanted to raise the gun at Meg, but I couldn't. She was my soul.

She sat there smiling with black lipstick on. It made her teeth look unnaturally white.

Her eyes were the opposite though. Consumed. Pitch.

Three boxes were arranged around her in the candlelight. Sophie's. Tracey's. Eric's. Three dead boxes for three dead teenagers. Three spirits inside Meg's body.

The air quivered with power.

"Do you want to know how I did it?" Meg smiled. "How I fooled everyone, even my best friend?"

This wasn't time for speeches though. There was only one word I needed now.

91

"Discedo!" I screamed, sending every ounce of rage and betrayal I felt at Meg.

The command thundered into her. A single spell smacked loose, clacking back into its box on the ground.

Yes! I'd done it!

The celebration was short lived.

Meg attacked, inhumanly fast, lashing out with a fist.

Her blow collided into my chest with a crack. I was sent spinning backward.

I expected pain but there was none. No splintered bones, just invincible protection.

I rolled and then sprung up.

But Meg was already on me, her hand on my throat.

She growled the word herself. "Disce-"

92

I smacked the gun into Meg's cheek, knocking the command from her lips.

She let me go, slumping to her knees.

The hiss from her throat was a chorus of demons. There was another whisper below it though.

Please, Lily, help.

I wouldn't be fooled twice. I kicked Meg in the chest. She fell back.

"Get out!" I screamed. "Out!"

My force of will propelled another spell clattering into a box.

Before I could continue, Meg took control.

"Out!" she moaned.

The last spell left at her weak command.

But I knew from Meg's thoughts this was far from over.

93

Before I could turn and run, an invisible force gripped me.

"No," Meg groaned from the ground.

"Yes," someone else whispered from the shadows.

It was the librarian, Mr Lombardi.

He melted from the darkness where he'd been hiding, controlling Meg using Cox's compulsion spell. I struggled to pull free of his influence. The gun I held dropped from my hand.

Lombardi's thoughts assaulted me, showing how he'd murdered the others. He'd attacked Cox for his power. Kidnapped Meg and forced spells into her, making her Fallen to be easier to control.

And now, he was going to kill me.

94

"I thought it was curious so many students wanted to read myths in Latin," Lombardi said in his soft, librarian's voice. "Then, I discovered the secret. So unfair that the rich and powerful are gifted even more power. What about us common people?"

He tilted his head, waiting for me to agree. I still couldn't move, so I spat at him.

"Yes, well, that's why you'll both die," he said, snapping his fingers. The spirits inside made me turn to Meg. "You're keeping the secret for yourselves too. Greedy, greedy."

Another finger snap and I stepped forward, raising my fists.

95

Meg cowered on the floor as I advanced. I struggled to resist, but the spirits inside me were strong. Lombardi had so much power over them.

I wanted to cry. It made me so angry. I wanted to scream.

I swung at Meg, who raised her hands to defend herself.

But, I didn't hit her.

Instead, I spun with the momentum, knocking the Spellkeepers next to Meg away.

They all rolled, clattering open.

Breathing in, I invited their power inside. "Welcome!"

Superhuman strength thrummed into me first. Then beauty. Then furious intelligence.

"I'm not Fallen yet," I growled at Lombardi.

96

I broke Lombardi's hold over me with a scream of stubborn will.

The five spells seething inside me roared with delight.

Lombardi spun, disappearing back into the shadows. The cloaking spells.

But I didn't need to see Lombardi to know he was there.

I had my whispers to guide me.

Zeroing in on his hateful mind, I ran forward, reaching into the darkness.

My fingers caught Lombardi's collar. I ripped him into the candlelight.

He tried to influence my spells again, but I batted the attempt away.

I was in control now, burning with power.

I *would not* be possessed.

I cracked Lombardi's temple with my powerful fist. His mind silenced. He dropped to the floor.

It was over. We'd done it.

Yet, magic still scorched through me. I was brimming with it. It needed to go somewhere.

I could feel all of the spells colliding inside. Burrowing deeper into my psyche and heart. It was too much. I couldn't control it.

I was getting hot. So hot.

One last shout of intelligence screamed at me. *Any more than three spells and you burn up.*

Five spirits had their hooks in me.

I heard a distant scream. Meg.

So hot.

98

Something deep inside wouldn't let me ignite. Maybe it was my stubborn streak. Maybe it was Meg's voice as she yelled at me to cast the spells off.

Whatever it was, I didn't burn.

Instead, I pushed the spirits away thudding back into their boxes.

Marcus and my original spells hung in the air, chilling the room with their dark energy. They tried to drift back toward me, but I willed them away.

Meg leapt up and hugged me tighter than she ever had. I hugged her back.

Lombardi groaned at our feet.

He wasn't dead, but he was finished.

99

Marcus arrived with the police not long after.

They cuffed Lombardi. When he came to, he raved about spells and how I was a witch with powers. That certainly wouldn't help his case in court.

I thought about what he'd said earlier though. That'd we'd been greedy keeping the spells secret. Maybe he was right.

But, he'd done so much worse.

"Is Cox okay?" I asked Marcus.

"He'll be fine," he said.

When the cops left, the three of us carefully collected the spells.

I wondered if I'd be allowed to keep mine.

I wondered if I even wanted to.

100

Cox grinned as I entered his hospital room.

"You held *five* spells inside you," was the first thing he said.

"Told you I was determined enough to use magic," I smiled.

"The Order visited. We debriefed on the whole ordeal." Cox nodded toward his bedside. "There's something on the table for you."

It was an old book. An eye blazed on the cover.

"The Order have agreed to train you themselves," Cox said.

I paused. That gift may be a curse.

I ran my fingers over the book. Perhaps it was time I wrote a new one of my own.

Acknowledgments

I'd like to say a big thank you to all of those who made this experimental little book possible.

Firstly, Sofia Behnke. Your professionalism as a young illustrator is, frankly, incredible. It was so amazing seeing Lily, Meg and Marcus come to life on the page (and screen) thanks to your wizardry.

To Sarah 'Pony' Bürvenich for your cover design and font knowledge. You're an absolute champion. I look forward to catching up in Melbourne one of these days soon.

To Alexis Orosa, your expert editing always adds something to my writing. I can't wait to work with you on more stuff.

To Charlie Bewley, my infernal collaborator and enabler, cheers for helping add some working-class grit to the voices of these characters, and helping me out with the nuances of highschool life in the UK. Nice one, bruva.

To all of those absolute lords who first supported this weird idea on Kickstarter and made it a reality. This thing wouldn't have happened without you. A special thanks to the Art Collector supporters, Francesca Manzini, Seamus Sands, Kohen Grogan, and Z. You're the best!

Finally, to Tara, for being my biggest supporter (and critic). I love you to the end of the galaxy and back. Always.

ABOUT TIM HAWKEN

Tim Hawken is a literary hooligan from Western Australia who writes dark sci-fi and fantasy. He is a 2-times winner of the AHWA's Flash Fiction Competition, has been shortlisted for an Australian Shadows Award, and likes to add a twist of wicked humour to his work.

Tim posts a 100-word, art-inspired story most days on Instagram (@tim_hawken).

ABOUT SOFIA BEHNKE

Sofia Behnke is an illustrator from the USA whose clean style and eye for lighting has seen her gain a solid following on social media. First recognised by authors like Holly Black, VE Schwab and Leigh Bardugo for her fan art, this is Sofia's commercial debut.

You can connect with Sofia at @behnsi on Instagram and @behnsii on Tiktok.